lauren child

Snow is my FAVORITE and my best

dial books for young readers

Charlie and Lola™

Text based on script written by Samantha Hill

Illustrations from the TV animation produced by Tiger Aspect

First published in the United States by
DIAL BOOKS FOR YOUNG READERS
A division of Penguin Young Readers Group
Published by The Penguin Group
Penguin Group (USA) Inc., 375 Hudson Street, New York, NY 10014, U.S.A.
Penguin Group (Canada), 90 Eglinton Avenue East, Suite 700, Toronto, Ontario, Canada M4P 2Y3 (a division of Pearson Penguin Canada Inc.)
Penguin Books Ltd, 80 Strand, London WC2R 0RL, England
Penguin Ireland, 25 St. Stephen's Green, Dublin 2, Ireland (a division of Penguin Books Ltd)
Penguin Group (Australia), 250 Camberwell Road, Camberwell, Victoria 3124, Australia (a division of Pearson Australia Group Pty Ltd)
Penguin Books India Pvt Ltd, 11 Community Centre, Panchsheel Park, New Delhi - 110 017, India
Penguin Group (NZ), Cnr Airborne and Rosedale Roads, Albany, Auckland 1310, New Zealand (a division of Pearson New Zealand Ltd)
Penguin Books (South Africa) (Pty) Ltd, 24 Sturdee Avenue, Rosebank, Johannesburg 2196, South Africa
Penguin Books Ltd, Registered Offices: 80 Strand, London WC2R 0RL, England
Published in Great Britain by Puffin Books

Manufactured in China on acid-free paper
1   3   5   7   9   10   8   6   4   2
Library of Congress Cataloging-in-Publication Data
Snow is my favorite and my best / Lauren Child.
p.   cm.—(Charlie and Lola)
ISBN 0-8037-3174-4
I. Title. II. Series: Child, Lauren. Charlie and Lola.
PZ7.C4383Sno 2006 • 2006005427

I have this little sister Lola.
She is small and very funny.
Today Lola is extremely excited
because the man on the weather
says it's going to snow.

Lola cannot wait for the snow to come.
She says, "Snow is my favorite
and is my best."

I say, "Remember, Lola,
Snow can only come when it is very, very cold.
Dad said it might not snow until midnight.
Or even tomorrow."

"I know,"
says Lola,
"but it is **extremely**
very **cold** right **now**.
So I think the
snow will come
sooner rather
than **midnight**."

At bedtime, Lola says,
"Do you think it has
started Snowing now, Charlie?"

"No, go to sleep, Lola."

She says, "I can't because
it might come while
I'm asleep, sleeping.

"I'll just do one more
check . . .
No Snow.
Not yet."

"See?" I say.
"Go to **sleep**."

But a little bit later
I hear Lola creeping
out of bed again.

"Ooooh!" she says.
"It's **Snowing!**
Charlie, come quick.
It's **Snowing**, it's really,
really Snowing!"

So I watch the **snow** with Lola.
She says, "Can we **go out**
and **play** in it **now**?"

"Not **now**, Lola," I say. "Wait until morning.
Then there'll be **more** and we can
go on the **sled** with Marv and Sizzles.
And **you** can build a **snowman** if you want."

In the morning,
Lola shouts,

"Charlie!
Get up, Charlie!
Mum! Dad!

It's all gone
extremely white!"

So Mum and Dad take us to
the park, and Lola is right,
everything has turned **extremely**,
completely **white**.

Then we see Marv and Lotta.
And I say, "Where's Sizzles?"

"Yes," says Lola, "where's Sizzles?"

Marv points to a small pile of snow.
"He's here!"
he says. "Look!"

Lotta and Lola
make snow angels.

Lola says,
"Snow
is my
favorite
and my
best."

"I love **snow!**" says Lotta. "It's my **best** too."

Then we find a big hill and we all
go on the sled. Even Sizzles!

I say, "Ready?
Steady?
Go!"

Wheeeeeeee

eeeeee!

Then me and Marv
    build a **snowman**.

Lotta says,
    "Let's make a
    Snow doggy,
        come on, Lola!"

Later we go home to have some hot chocolate.
Marv says, "Mmmm. I love hot chocolate!"
Lola says,
"I love snow. Tomorrow I might put snowdog
and Sizzles on the sled for a ride."

"I'm going to make a snow kennel," says Lotta,
". . . and what about snow puppies?"

"Yes!" says Lola. "We can have lots of snow puppies!"

But when we go to the park the next day,
Lola can't make anything.

"It's gone!" she says.
"All the lovely snow is absolutely gone.
There's no more white, Charlie.
It's all cold
and wet
and brown.
And snowdog's gone."

So we go home again.

Lola says,
"Why can't we
        have **snow**
   every day?"

And I say,
"Because it wouldn't be **special**.
Imagine you had a **birthday**
every day, so you had **parties**
and **cakes** and **presents**
all the time."

And Lola says,
"What's **wrong** with having
birthdays every day?"

And I say,
"It wouldn't be a **treat**, would it? I'm not
sure you would like **snow every** day."

"I **would**, Charlie," says Lola.
"**Snow** is my **favorite**
and is my **best**."

Then I have a really good idea.

"Well, imagine a completely white land . . .

. . . where it's **snowy** and **cold every** day.
It's called the **Arctic**."

"Look at the **polar bear**," says Lola.
"What's he doing, Charlie?"
I say, "He's going for a **swim**."

"I'd like to go **swimming**," says Lola.
"Where's the **beach**?"
I say,
"There isn't a **beach**, Lola.
It's far too **cold** for us to go **swimming**."

Then I say, "And then there's this place right at the bottom of the world called the **Antarctic**, where you get seals and whales and . . . . .

"Penguins!" says Lola.
"Don't the penguins look smart,
Charlie! They look like they're
going to a party!
I wish I was wearing my best smartest
party dress, you know, the stripy one."

And I say,
"You couldn't wear your stripy dress in the Antarctic.
You have to wear your coat all the time,
because it's so cold."

"Oh yes," says Lola, "I forgot."

Then I say, "But when it's all snowy, you can do this . . .

. . . says, "but can we go home now?"

And I say, "But why? I thought snow was your favorite and was your best!"

come on!"

And I say, "Isn't it amazing?" "Wow!" says Lola.

And we slide on the ice with the penguins.

"Yes, Charlie," she...

Lola says, "I do like it, Charlie. But I'm just a bit chilly!

"Snow is my **favorite** and my **best**, Charlie," says Lola, "but if it was **snowy all** the time there would be lots of things you **couldn't** do. So we're maybe lucky, we can do **swimming** and have **stripy** dresses **and** have **snow.**

"But I do feel **sad** that the **snow** has all **gone.**

So I say,

"I've got a

surprise for you.
Don't **peek!**"

Lola says,
"A teeny weeny snowman
who lives in the **freezer!**
How did he get in there?"

"I don't know!" I say.

Lola says, "He's me|ting!"
I say, "Shall I put him back
in the freezer so we can keep him?"
"Oh no, Charlie," says Lola.
"Let's watch him me|t!"